# JUST LOST!

## BY GINA AND MERCER MAYER

*For Matthew &
Lauren Atkinson*

**A GOLDEN BOOK • NEW YORK**

Western Publishing Company, Inc., Racine, Wisconsin 53404

Library of Congress Catalog Card Number: 93-73533 ISBN: 0-307-12844-X/ISBN: 0-307-62844-2 (lib. bdg.)   A  MCMXCIV

Mom took us shopping at the mall. There were a jillion critters there.

I wanted to push my brother's stroller,
but the mall was just too crowded.
Mom pushed him instead.

There was such a big crowd that I could barely see anything. Mom said, "Stay close by me so you won't get lost."

When we were right in the middle of the
crowd, I noticed that my shoe was untied.
I tied it so I wouldn't trip.

When I stood up, I couldn't find Mom.
I climbed up on a bench to look around.

TOY

I yelled, "MOM!"
But it was so noisy,
no one could hear me.

My mom was lost at the mall!

I wanted to cry, but I didn't.
I was brave instead.

I didn't know what to do,
so I went to the toy store.

The store clerk said, "May I help you?"
I said, "My mom is lost!"

She said, "Don't worry, we'll find her for you." She called a security guard on the store phone.

The clerk let me play with some toys while we waited for the security guard to arrive.

The security guard was wearing
a uniform. He looked like a policeman.
"You can come to my office until
we find your mom," he said.

He let me wear his hat.

I felt really cool walking through the mall with a security guard.

The security office was a small room.
There were lots of TV sets showing
everything at the mall.

I saw a critter crying.
I guess she didn't want
to leave the toy store.

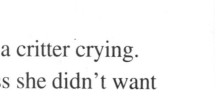

I saw critters reading
in the bookstore.

I saw critters eating
in the restaurants.

But none of them could see me.
It was like being a real spy.

The security guard made an announcement over the loudspeaker: "Little Critter's mom, please come to the security office to pick him up."

Then he gave me a doughnut and some juice. He let me look through the Lost and Found box.

All of a sudden I saw my mom on one of the TV screens. She was walking through the mall with another security guard. I said, "There she is—that's my mom!"

The office door opened.
Mom and my brother and sister came in.

Mom looked worried. I guess she's just not
as brave as me. She said, "I was so worried."
I said, "I was really brave. I didn't even cry."
Then Mom smiled and said, "I'm very
proud of you, Little Critter."
I knew she was glad
I found them.

The next time we go to the mall
I'm going to be really careful.
Mom just hates getting lost at the mall.